WHEN
THE RAIN CAME

Presented to

Simon Fraser

From: A.P.C.

Sunday School.
1998

CHRISTIAN ART
TEL: 01323 410930

WHEN
THE RAIN CAME

Eleanor Watkins

CHRISTIAN FOCUS PUBLICATIONS

© 1996 Eleanor Watkins
ISBN 1-85792-210-7

Published by
Christian Focus Publications Ltd
Geanies House, Fearn, Ross-shire,
IV20 1TW, Scotland, Great Britain

Cover design by Donna Macleod
Cover illustration by Mike Italiaander, Allied Artists

Printed and bound in Great Britain by
Cox & Wyman Ltd, Reading, Berks

Contents

Chapter One

Michael

Michael was packing his bag for the tenth or eleventh time, stuffing in his favourite video, a snorkel and football boots. Carol smiled when she came into the room with an armful of clean sheets.

'It's only for the weekend, Mike, not six months!'

Michael smiled back, a little uncertainly. Carol was his favourite among the helpers, slim and pretty, with pink cheeks and shiny brown hair. She often found time to watch TV with him or play a quick card game.

'I know, but I might need these things. You never know what we'll be doing. I'd better take them just in case.'

He zipped up the bulging bag with some difficulty. 'What time is it, Carol?'

'About two minutes since you last asked.' She looked at her watch. 'Quarter to ten. You've got half an hour. Why don't you go and play outside for a while?'

'I might get messed up,' said Michael. He sat on the neatly made bed, chin in hands. 'Do you think they like me, really, Carol?'

Carol paused. She knew he wanted reassurance, but she'd seen so many boys like him who'd been disappointed. She said, 'I'm sure they do, Mike. And I hope you have lots of fun this weekend.' She rumpled his straight fair hair and said, 'I've got to go. I'm off at ten.'

Michael felt his anxiety change to resentment. He hated the way different staff came on and went off, just when you were trying to tell them something, or in the middle of a game with one of them. Even the Social Workers changed far too often for his liking. But there was nothing he could do about it.

'Well, I'll tell you all about it on Monday,' he said.

Carol stopped, her hand on the door handle. 'Oh, Mike - didn't you know? I'm not coming back. I'm getting married next week - to Tim. I thought everyone knew that.'

She looked pleased and excited, her eyes shining and her cheeks pinker than ever. Michael had a queer feeling, as though he'd been punched in the stomach. He hadn't realised just how fond he'd grown of Carol since she'd worked at the Home. And now she was going away, marrying Tim, whoever he was. Tears sprang into his eyes and he lowered his head.

Carol slipped back to kiss him quietly on the cheek. 'Goodbye, Mike. I hope everything works out for you. And remember, God loves you. He's your Father and you can always trust him.'

Alone, he fought the tears for a few moments. He didn't want Carol to marry Tim. If she wanted to marry someone, he'd have married her himself when he grew up. You'd think she could have waited a few years! It wasn't fair! There was nobody he could depend on, not one! He had a longing, suddenly, to fling himself on the bed, and cry for Mum.

But it was a long time since he'd done that. He gulped once or twice and blinked hard. He decided, after all, it might be a good idea to wait in the garden for the Merediths to arrive. Then he'd be sure to see them the moment their car turned in the drive.

It was going to be a glorious October day. Already the morning mist had cleared and the leaves of the plum trees were yellow on the grass. The little kids were playing on the swings and a couple of small girls fussed about with a doll's pram. Most of the boys his age had gone swimming for the morning, but Dean Patterson appeared from somewhere and approached him. Michael turned away, trying to avoid Dean, but the bigger boy caught up, peering knowingly into Michael's face.

'Thought you were going away for the weekend.'

'I am. I'm just waiting to be fetched.'

'Bet they won't come. They've probably changed their mind. Nobody would want you, I shouldn't think.'

Michael didn't answer. Dean was a bully and he was sly with it, pinching and tweaking when you least expected it and where it hurt most. Michael wished he had the courage to thump him, but Dean was eleven to his nine-and-a-half years, and big and strong for his age.

'Anyway, I'm off myself for the weekend,' boasted Dean. 'My Mum's coming a bit later and we're going to stay in a big motel. A motel's a place you drive to in your car, and you have a nice place all to yourself.'

'I know that,' said Michael.

'You don't know anything,' said Dean crushingly. 'Anyway, the one we're going to is the poshest in the country. You can ring room service for anything you want, and there's a telly and video in every room. We're going shopping in London. My Mum's getting a gold watch for herself, and a CD player for me.'

Michael didn't for a moment believe any of this, but

force of habit made him reply, 'Bet she isn't. Anyway, that's no big deal. My Mum's got lots of expensive jewellry.

'Bet she hasn't. Anyway, my Mum's buying herself another watch, for good, so she can use the old one just for everyday. And she's getting me a brand new mountain bike.'

Dean's mother had never, to Michael's knowledge, bought Dean so much as a pair of socks, and hardly ever visited him. As for his own mother - well, he hadn't seen her for a long time either, and the thought of her was so painful that he mostly tried not to. Deep down, he wondered why he and Dean played this silly game. Both of them knew perfectly well it was all talk.

Yet when Dean said, 'My Mum's picking me up in her new car. It's brand new - a Ferrari,' he found himself replying at once, 'Well, my Mum's got a new car, too. A Jaguar. She's picking me up in it this morning.'

Dean pounced triumphantly. 'She can't be, 'cos you said those other people were taking you home for the weekend. You're a liar!'

Michael floundered. 'I'm not. They *are* coming for me, if... if Mum can't make it.'

'Bet they won't come. Anyway, they won't want you once they find out you wet the bed.'

Michael cringed. Nothing of this nature could be kept a secret at Woodcroft House. He had been worried on this score himself, though it happened much less often these days, and Mrs Hall had promised she'd have a word with the Merediths.

Dean's face loomed near, sneering and chanting.

'Michael Scott wets the bed! Michael Scott wets the bed!'

Michael was suddenly furious. His knuckles tingled with the urge to hit Dean. He tried to work out the distance to the side door, wondering if he could get in one good thump and then make it to safety before Dean recovered. He would suffer for it on Monday, but it might be worth it.

While he was still weighing it up, a car turned into the drive, not a Ferrari or a Jaguar, but a very ordinary blue Ford Cortina. Michael saw that the driver was Mr Meredith, with Mrs Meredith beside him and the children, Edward and Susan, in the back seat.

He turned triumphantly to Dean, his anger ebbing away. 'See! It's them! They've come to pick me up.'

And he was pleased to note that for once Dean had nothing to say in reply.

Chapter Two

Tom

Miss Murgatroyd, the teacher of 6M, had begun the day with a slight headache, which grew worse as the day progressed. She had overslept, skipped breakfast and been late for school, which she prided herself hardly ever happened. During the lunch hour she'd had to rush to the Medical Centre with a child who'd crashed into another in the playground and gashed its cheek. This meant she'd had to gobble her lunch, which had given her twinges of indigestion. Altogether, Miss Murgatroyd could feel herself becoming crabby and bad-tempered as afternoon classes began.

However, she tried not to let it show. Miss Murgatroyd considered herself to be a good teacher and a fair one. The head himself had told her more than once that her discipline was better than that of any other class in the school. She felt that this was no mean achievement, for some of the pupils in class 6M, she felt, were badly out of control and in need of a firm hand by the time they came to her.

Miss Murgatroyd couldn't help feeling that today's standards left much to be desired. Especially among the boys. She had quite a soft spot for little girls, difficult though some were, but the boys often brought her to the brink of despair. Other people, she felt, would have by now accepted early retirement and thankfully left today's boy pupils to someone younger and fitter.

This afternoon, the class were making silhouettes, drawing each other's profiles and cutting out the shape in black paper, which was then pasted on to a vividly-coloured background. She planned to pin up the finished work on the classroom wall for a striking frieze effect. Miss Murgatroyd's head throbbed, and by mid-afternoon she was obliged to leave the room to take two aspirins and a glass of water in the staffroom.

She was gone for less than two minutes. On her return she sensed at once that mischief was afoot. A group of boys were bunched around a table. And in the centre of the group she saw a familiar brown head.

'Tom!' she said sharply. 'Get on with your painting, please.'

Tom Kent's large hazel eyes looked innocently up at her. 'I've finished, miss. Look!' he held up his paper background, coloured in bright vermilion. 'I'm just waiting for it to dry, before sticking the silhouette on.'

Miss Murgatroyd felt slightly exasperated. Tom was something of a trial to her, a bundle of restless energy that kept him forever on the move. What a change from his sister, Lucy, who'd been in her class two years before and was such a sweet child, hard-working and sunny-natured. Not that Tom wasn't charming, too, in his way, when he chose to be. But he was also one of those children who are the teacher's scourge - bright as a button and well able to keep ahead of the work. At the same time, he managed to be at the centre of any mischief going on, and a great distraction to the other pupils.

She sighed. 'Yes - well, don't crowd together like that.'

The others moved apart, and she could see what they'd

been looking at. Tom had built four or five of the small jars of poster paint into a little tower, across which he had placed a ruler. On each end of the ruler were placed two more jars of paint, balanced precariously. Tom had been just about to add a drop or two of water to one of the top jars. Seeing the teacher stare aghast, he explained brightly, 'I was just seeing how much paint it takes to balance these jars. This one needs...'

'Tom...' began Miss Murgatroyd warningly.

But it was too late. Someone nudged the table, just a touch, accidentally or on purpose. It was enough to bring the whole construction crashing down. Sloppy wet paint flew everywhere, spattering papers, tables, floors and walls. A couple of jars smashed, one of the girls shrieked, and the dull throb in Miss Murgatroyd's temples became acute pain.

There was silence for a moment. Every one of the thirty-two boys and girls stared expectantly at their teacher. Miss Murgatroyd struggled with an urge to take Tom Kent by the neck and throttle him. Then the bell rang, signalling the end of the lesson, and of the school day. Miss Murgatroyd dismissed the children but some of them hovered, anxious to go yet reluctant to miss her reaction to the incident. Tom was making for the door.

'Tom!' said Miss Murgatroyd sharply. 'Wait, please.'

He came back and stood before her enquiringly. 'Yes, miss?'

'Haven't you anything to say?'

He looked puzzled for a moment, until his eye fell on the mess of spilt paint and broken glass. 'Oh! Yes, miss. Sorry, miss.'

He was poised, ready for flight. Not yet, Mr Tom

Kent, thought Miss Murgatroyd. She said in a reasonable tone, 'Since you were responsible for this mess, I think you ought to help clear it up. It's hardly fair to leave it to the cleaning lady.'

A flicker of alarm clouded Tom's eyes.

'But, miss, I've got football practice at four...'

'That,' said Miss Murgatroyd calmly, 'is your problem. I shall be late too, and that's mine. Now get a damp cloth and start on the walls.'

For a moment he stared rebelliously. Then he grinned with such unexpected charm that she could understand why he was so popular. 'Okay, miss.'

The phone rang and was answered by the cleaning lady, who called out, 'Miss Murgatroyd! It's for you!'

She left Tom taking wet swipes at the wall and went to answer it. In spite of herself, she felt a smile touch her lips. Impossible boy! Despite everything, one couldn't help liking him. He certainly needed a firm hand, though.

When she returned, Tom was working his way round the classroom, leaving the walls wet and smeary but passable. He gave her a grin that bore no malice, and her spirits lifted. Her headache was beginning to ease at last, and tomorrow was another day. And with careful handling, she'd make something of Tom Kent yet.

She swept up the bits of glass and wrapped them carefully, dumped them in the bin and mopped the floor. Tom had just a few more splotches to remove. Miss Murgatroyd sat down at her desk for a moment's rest while he finished.

A strangely damp sensation began to seep through her clothing. She got up, and discovered a sheet of drawing paper stuck to the rear of her beige skirt. Peeled off, it left a rectangle of bright, wet, orange paint. Her head began to throb again.

'Tom!'

His back, as he rubbed industriously at the last blob, seemed the picture of innocence. He turned and straightened up, blinking. 'Yes, miss?'

The sheet of paper on her chair could have been an accident, she supposed, although the paint seemed strangely fresh. It would take ages to remove the stain from her skirt. Suddenly she felt very tired.

'Thank you, Tom,' she said. 'You can go home now.'

Chapter Three

Home

Tom burst through the front door, red-faced and untidy, having run all the way home. He plunged at once into the hall cupboard and began to scrabble about.

'Tom!'

Mum appeared at the kitchen doorway, cheeks flushed with flour on her hands. Good, thought Tom, that means she's making something with pastry. He grinned and returned to the cupboard. 'Mum, where's my other football boot? I'm going to be late for practice.'

'Tom!'

Mum could sound quite like Miss Murgie when she spoke like that. 'You're almost half an hour late. I want to know why.'

He sighed, his head still in the cupboard. 'Miss Murgatroyd kept me behind. Some paint got spilt and I had to clear it up.' He didn't mention the wet paint on Miss Murgatroyd's chair. After all, it had been an accident, or almost. He'd found the sheet someone had left behind and put it on the chair out of the way. He'd never intended her to sit down on it, though it *had* crossed his mind that she *might*. Anyway, if Mum learned about that she would be sure to make him apologise. Maybe he would, in any case, poor old Murgie had looked very weary.

What on earth had happened to that boot?

'You really should be more careful,' said Mum with a

sigh. 'By the way, we've got something to tell you. Duane will be coming on Friday evening - for good, this time.'

Tom emerged for a moment, hot and tousled. 'Oh, great! Cool! Mum - where *is* my boot? Oh, I've got it - bye, Mum! I've got to go and get changed.'

He bolted for the stairs. Tidying the disarranged cupboard and closing the door behind him, his mother gave a rueful smile. When would Tom learn to take life at anything less than breakneck speed?

Upstairs in his room, Tom digested her piece of news as he flung off his clothes and pulled on his track suit. So Duane was really coming for good at last! He remembered that first time Mum and Dad had sat down with him and Lucy to discuss the possibility of taking a foster child to live with them. Mum and Dad belonged to an organisation which he always thought of as 'sign-off'. It was really spelt CINOF, and meant Children In Need Of Families. Every so often, newsletters came through the post with pictures and news of children - boys and girls, big and small, black and white - all needing families to belong to. Mum and Dad felt that perhaps they could foster a child through CINOF.

'What do you think?' Dad had asked when they'd explained a little, looking at Tom and Lucy.

Twelve-year old Lucy had clasped her hands, blue eyes shining. 'Oh, I think it's a wonderful idea! Those poor little children! I'll help you look after it, Mum. I'll read to it and tuck it up in bed. The poor little thing will be so pleased to have a proper home!'

She burst into tears, quite overcome.

Tom gave her a glance of scorn. Lucy was always bursting into tears these days. They used to be great pals, but lately she'd got boring and was only interested in things like painting her nails pink and her eyelids green - or sometimes even the other way round - trying on clothes and giggling for hours on the phone with her girlfriends. She read soppy girls magazines and love stories, weeping gallons of tears over the sad bits. Altogether she had become a great embarrassment to her brother.

Mum passed her a tissue. 'Tom?' said Dad. 'What do you think?'

Tom hadn't been quite sure at first. Gradually though, the thought of having a little brother grew on him. He'd be able to teach him football and cricket and roller-skating, look after him at school and stick up for him if he needed it. His last doubts had been dispelled altogether when, after endless interviews and meetings, they at last met Duane.

Duane was five years old, chubby, coffee-coloured and cheerful. He talked and chattered non-stop, ate vast amounts of food and was inclined to show off and take hair-raising risks. Tom felt he and Duane had a great deal in common. They had visited him at his short-term foster home, and taken him out at weekends. They were all exhausted after a day at a theme park with him, and exhausted again after they'd taken him to a funfair. He'd spent two weekends with them, and attached himself particularly to Tom, whom he looked up to and admired very much.

And now Duane was coming home for good. Tom paused for a moment and glanced round the bedroom, neat when he'd entered it, now strewn with his discarded clothing. Mum had given the room a good turn-out and installed a new bed in the opposite corner to his. She'd made matching covers in a yellow material with racing cars, and bought two new green rugs. They'd even put a little bookcase beside Duane's bed and filled it with Tom's old Rupert Bear, Winnie the Pooh and Beatrix Potter books for Duane to look at.

And after Friday, Duane would be there for good, sleeping in that bed. Tom felt a strange sense of contentment. Little brothers could be a nuisance, but on the whole they were nice to have. He'd take good care of Duane.

But just now, he was getting later and later for football practice. Leaving his belongings lying where they'd fallen, he took the stairs two at a time, and headed for the front door.

Chapter Four

At the Merediths'

'Michael,' said Mrs Meredith, appearing at the door of the sitting room. 'I have to go out unexpectedly - an emergency committee meeting. Will you be alright for a while? My husband's golfing, Susan's out and Edward's gone to the library but he'll be back soon. There's a cheese salad for lunch.'

Michael looked up from the Saturday morning TV show he'd been watching. Mrs Meredith, tall and thin with glasses, had her usual slightly distracted expression. She was always rushing off to some meeting or other, to do with Animal Rights or CND or Friends of the Earth, or some other good cause. She had turned out to be quite a surprise to Michael, who expected proper mothers to be people who mainly stayed in the kitchen cooking or ironing.

In fact, none of the Merediths were anything like he'd expected. Mr Meredith worked long hours at his office, and was too tired in the evenings to do more than read the paper or watch TV. Fourteen-year old Susan wanted to be a model, and was obsessed with her appearance, and, most of all, her diet. Edward was perhaps the biggest disappointment of all, being what Michael called a swot, with his head always in a book and no interest in sport.

But they were a family and they'd accepted him as part of it, and that was all that mattered.

'Yes, I'll be alright,' said Michael.

Mrs Meredith departed with a rattle of big wooden beads, and he was alone in the house. The TV show came to an end and he switched off the set and climbed to his feet. Sunshine slanted into the room, showing a film of dust on the furniture. Mrs Meredith didn't bother too much with housework, feeling that it was unimportant and time-consuming. The family did not seem to mind, though sometimes they complained if there were no clean shirts or socks.

Wandering into the kitchen, Michael noticed that the breakfast dishes hadn't been washed either. He was hungry again already, and investigated the cupboards hopefully. The sultana bran, muesli and wholewheat bread did not appeal to him. What he really fancied was a bag of crisps and a chocolate bar. But Mrs Meredith didn't allow junk food, and fed them mainly on healthy salads, brown rice and pasta and wholegrain cereals. She was a vegetarian herself.

Michael didn't think the family shared her views, for he had noticed that Mr Meredith often ate at the golf club, and one day he had spied a whole lot of chocolate wrappers and crisp packets under Edward's bed. Susan seemed to eat hardly at all, and he himself managed to survive by nipping to the chip shop on the corner as soon as they opened on a Saturday afternoon, and gobbling pie and chips on the way home. It made a big hole in his pocket money, but it kept him from starving.

Michael considered washing the breakfast dishes. It was Susan's turn really, he knew, but he didn't mind doing a good turn for her. Susan was very pretty, and was kind to him when she noticed him, which wasn't often, because she was usually in her room with her head in a fashion magazine. But there seemed to be so many dishes, with blobs of cold cereal already set hard on the bowls, and a lot of coffee mugs. He'd leave them for a bit and do them later, perhaps, if nothing better turned up. This was his third weekend with the Merediths, and the first time he'd ever been alone in the house. He might as well have a nose around while he had the chance.

Edward's room was very untidy, with banana and orange peel as well as the paper wrappers, clothes and books strewn all over the floor. Michael noticed some forbidden weirdo comics half hidden among them. The children were expected to keep their own rooms in order, and didn't make much of a job of it, he thought. Susan's was perhaps a shade neater, with garments festooning the cupboard door and strings of beads hanging over the long mirror. Little tubes and bottles, sticks and palettes of make-up littered the dressing table. Michael noticed two or three plates of food, hardly touched, pushed out of sight, under the chest of drawers and on a high shelf. One of them had green hairy things growing on it and looked as though it had been there for a very long time. He pulled a face.

His own room was the neatest of the lot, though maybe that was because he only slept in it for one night a week.

He had never been into Mr and Mrs Meredith's bedroom before, and felt a little daring as he entered. It had folkweave curtains and bedspread in the kind of ethnic design that Mrs Meredith seemed so fond of. The furniture was large and antique, and a large collection of china bells stood on the dressing table.

Intrigued, Michael went over to take a closer look at the bells. They were of all shapes and sizes, from tiny delicate ones to large, handsome fluted and flared ones with wooden handles. Some had pictures painted on the china, flowers in delicate colours or trailing ivy, and one had a brightly-coloured Christmas scene of robins and holly. When Michael gingerly picked one up, a little clapper inside tinkled daintily.

All the bells had different notes, depending on their size and the thickness of the china. Michael picked them up and tinkled them one by one, replacing them carefully. But when he tried the Christmas bell he found that it wouldn't tinkle at all. He turned it upside down, holding it up to see if the clapper was stuck or perhaps missing. Next moment, the bell had somehow slipped through his fingers and crashed on to the top of the dressing table. Michael stared in horror. The Christmas bell lay on the wood surface, broken into maybe a dozen pieces of china. Its bright robins and holly were shattered and fragmented. His heart began to thump hard with guilt and fear. It had been an accident, but he'd had no business to be poking around in the Merediths' bedroom and meddling with their things. What on earth was he going to say to them? Frantically he wondered whether he could stick the pieces together again with Superglue or something, so that they wouldn't notice.

There was a thump of the front door closing behind someone and footsteps in the hall. Edward was back from the library. In a panic, he scooped the broken china pieces into his hand, pushing the bells from either side of it closer together to hide the gap. He slipped out of the room, closed the door quietly behind him, and crept across the landing to his own room. There he hurriedly pushed the pieces into his sports bag, covered them with his spare socks and sweatshirt, and zipped the bag up tight.

Chapter Five

Disappointments

'It was an accident,' Michael blurted out.

He stood in the office facing Miss Hall's desk, his hands gripped painfully together in front of him.

Miss Hall frowned at him over her spectacles in a puzzled way. 'An accident? What do you mean, Michael?'

'The bell,' said Michael desperately. 'The little china bell that I broke - it was an accident. I didn't mean to drop it. It just slipped.'

Miss Hall looked mystified. 'A china bell? I don't know anything about that. What are you talking about?'

Michael looked at her. He couldn't believe that she didn't know about the bell. He had listened to what she had told him when she'd called him into the office. She'd said that Susan Meredith was very ill in hospital with some illness with a strange name, that was something to do with losing weight and being too thin - slimmer's disease, it was sometimes called, she said. It meant that Mr and Mrs Meredith wouldn't be able to have him for weekends any more, at least, not for the present.

He only half understood and didn't believe the story at all. Susan's illness was just an excuse, he thought bitterly. The Merediths were saying, in a kind way, that they didn't want him any more because he was a meddler and a thief, someone not to be trusted.

He blinked back the tears. 'I - I bust a china bell in their bedroom. Last Saturday. It was an accident. It slipped. I brought it back to see if I could get it mended. It's still upstairs in my bag...'

Miss Hall was looking at him kindly but with a touch of exasperation. It had been a rather trying day. 'Michael, they've mentioned nothing about any bell. It was silly of you to hide it like that. They'd have understood if you'd explained, I'm sure. I thought I'd made it clear to you that the reason they can't have you is because of Susan's anorexia...'

Michael didn't hear the rest. The tears flowed over and squeezed out on to his cheeks. He turned and ran from the room, clattering across the tiled hall and up the stairs. Mercifully, the upstairs was deserted at this time in the evening, everyone was watching TV or doing homework. He reached the bedroom and flung himself face down on his bed. Despair flooded through him like a dark tide. He wouldn't be going to the Merediths' ever again. All his hope of finding a family had once again been snatched away. He forgot all his complaints about the Meredith family - Mrs Meredith's awful food, Mr Meredith's grumpiness, and the fact that he and Edward didn't like the same kind of things. They were a family, and for a few hopeful weeks he'd thought he might be a part of it too, for good. Now the dream was shattered, just like so many other of his dreams.

For several minutes he sobbed with his head buried in the pillow. His mother wouldn't ever take him home - he knew that, though sometimes he wouldn't let himself admit it. No one wanted him, not really. The things that Dean Patterson said about him were quite true. He had no-one in the world to depend on.

Suddenly, into his mind popped the words Carol had said just before she left. 'You can always trust God!'

Carol talked as though God was real to her, someone she knew. She'd said God was his Father, though he didn't really understand. He didn't have a real father, but he thought that fathers were supposed to take care of you. The people who'd taken care of him were mainly social workers and houseparents, and all too often they let you down. A real father wouldn't let you down, would he?

A little quieter, he rolled over on to his back and rubbed his eyes with grimy knuckles. Carol said you could talk to God and that he'd always hear. And he trusted Carol, as much as he trusted anyone .

'God,' he said forlornly in the empty room. 'I'm fed up with all this. I don't know what to do. Nobody wants me. I wish you'd help me - if you're real.'

He didn't know whether God was supposed to speak back, in a booming voice or something, but what happened was nothing at all. Just silence, except for the noise of the water pipes in the bathroom opposite, which always gurgled when someone turned on a tap downstairs. Worn out, Michael pulled the eiderdown over his head and fell asleep.

* * *

Tom and Duane had worked hard at the bonfire all afternoon, dragging branches, twigs, hoarded rubbish and even a couple of old tyres to the patch of waste grown at the end of the orchard where the bonfire was always built.

'Tyres make lovely smoke, thick and black - it nearly chokes you,' said Tom with satisfaction.

Duane's chocolate-brown eyes were sparkling with excitement. He wore a red bobble hat and new red wellingtons that Mum and Lucy had bought for him on their last shopping expedition. Both of them, especially Lucy, loved buying clothes and dressing Duane up in them. Tom had no patience with all this. But Duane put up with it all, with no more than the odd sigh or wriggle of protest. He was sunny-natured and eager to please, especially with Tom, whom he greatly admired and modelled himself upon.

Duane was dragging a dead apple branch bigger than himself, to feed the fire. He paused, breathless. 'Shall I put it here, Tom?'

Tom considered. 'No, bring it round to this side. The fire's getting a bit lop-sided.'

Duane obeyed him importantly, trotting round the piled wood and rubbish. They heaved the branch into position. It balanced up the bonfire nicely. Tom folded his arms and looked at it with satisfaction. Duane folded his arms too. Tom scratched his ear. Duane scratched his. It was a nice change to be admired, thought Tom. He patted Duane's head kindly, and said, 'Let's go and get the Guy.'

Lucy considered herself much too old for bonfires, but she had made a very lifelike Guy Fawkes from a straw-stuffed boiler suit, with ancient padded gloves on the ends of broomstick arms and an old peaked cap on the straw head.

'I bet she'll cry her eyes out when he goes up in smoke,' said Tom with a grin.

They were taking the Guy from the garden shed, carrying him between them like a body, with Tom at the head and Duane at the feet, when a call came from the house.

'Tom! Bring Duane and come here, please!'

Tom thought that Mum's voice sounded a bit odd. He took Duane's grubby hand. 'Let's go and see what's up.'

The sound of voices could be heard from the living room as they let themselves in. 'Boots off,' said Tom. 'We've got visitors.'

Suddenly, the living room door flew open and Lucy appeared. She stared tragically, first at Duane and then at Tom, opened her mouth to speak, but instead burst into tears and ran sobbing up the stairs.

'Tom?' called Mum as the boys stared perplexed after her. 'Come in please, and bring Duane.'

Her voice sounded tight and strained. Two ladies sat side by side on the sofa, drinking tea. One looked like a teacher or a social worker. The other was young with a short cropped hairstyle and long black boots. Tom noticed that her little finger stuck out as she drank her tea.

Mum's face was pale and set as she looked at the two boys standing side by side in the doorway.

'This is Tom,' she said to the two ladies. 'Tom, this is Miss Haines, a social worker, and - and this is Mrs Sharon Winston. She's Duane's mother.'

Chapter Six

A New Beginning

Christmas had come and gone, and another New Year had begun. It had been a disappointing Christmas, in many ways, thought Tom, in spite of the ace new computer he'd been given by his parents. Mum and Dad had tried hard to make it a happy time, but all of them, especially Lucy and himself, couldn't help thinking how different it would all have been if Duane had still been with them.

Tom still had a deep feeling of hurt whenever he thought of the cheeky, cheerful little brown-skinned boy who had been his small brother for so short a time. The other bed was still in the corner of his room, but he had taken away the Rupert Bear and Winnie-the-Pooh books, and the Lion King poster from the wall.

That afternoon when Duane's mother had turned up to call for her son, stayed in his mind like a bad dream. He remembered painfully every moment of the strained conversation in the living room. Sharon Winston - whom he privately thought of as a silly cow - had fussed and twittered over Duane, calling him her sugar plum and her tweetie-pie. She said silly things like she preferred his hair grown a little longer, and how he could do with some new, trendy clothes. The social worker had gone into long, involved explanations of Sharon's improved circumstances and changes in the fostering plan. Mum and Dad had looked pale, shocked and helpless. Most painful of all was the way that Duane had run straight to his mother, and later had walked off hand-in-hand with her, with never a backward glance for Tom and the family.

Tom sighed, rummaging in his drawer for a sweater. They were driving out to Woodcroft House this afternoon and he didn't want to go at all. He wasn't a bit keen on trying again with another boy, which was what Mum and Dad had decided on when they'd recovered a little and thought and talked and prayed. He neither liked nor disliked Michael, whom they'd met at the Home, and who was almost his own age, but he'd have preferred not to have him. There was nothing exactly wrong with Michael, except that he wasn't Duane, whom Tom still thought of as his little brother.

'Tom!' called Mum from below. 'Hurry up! We'll be late!'

Tom sighed, pulled his green sweatshirt over his head and thumped noisily down the stairs.

Although it was a cold January afternoon, Michael was waiting for them in the garden, clutching a bulging sports bag. This was to be his first weekend with Tom's family. A bigger pasty-faced boy was with him. He walked over with Michael as they climbed out of the car.

'Hello,' smiled the pasty-faced boy. 'I'm Dean Patterson. Would you like me to tell Miss Hall you're here?'

Mum and Dad seemed grateful and impressed. 'Thank you very much, Dean. That's kind of you.'

Tom saw that Michael hung back, scowling a little. He guessed that Michael didn't like Dean, and he didn't blame him, because he didn't think much of Dean himself. He seemed a bit of a creep. He felt a twinge of sympathy for Michael. He said, 'Hi, Michael. Did you remember your footie boots?'

Michael nodded eagerly, his pale cheeks flushing a little. They spoke briefly to Miss Hall and drove away, leaving Dean standing gazing after them. 'What a helpful boy,' said Mum. 'Is he your special friend, Mike?'

'Sort of,' said Michael uncomfortably. He was feeling nervous and keyed-up, desperately anxious that the weekend should be a success. Having another chance at a family was more than he'd expected, and he mustn't blow it this time.

Tom, whom Michael had found to be rather cold and aloof at their first meeting, seemed to be making an effort to be friendly.

'That's my school,' he said, when they had passed through the centre of town and come out on the other side.

Michael looked at the long, greyish building. 'Where's the football pitch?'

'We don't have one, not a proper one. We play in the yard with a chalked-out pitch. I have to go to the sports centre in town to train properly.'

To his own horror, Michael heard himself say, 'Our school has two pitches. With proper goals. I may be picked for the under-12s next year. We've got a boxing ring. And an indoor gym.'

Tom's friendly attitude seemed to cool. But he tried again when they passed the Leisure Centre. 'That's where I go swimming.'

'Is there a roller-skating rink?'

'Well... no...'

'I go roller-skating most Saturdays. I had to miss it

today because of going with you. Next year I may start karate classes.'

Michael listened to himself with a kind of despair, yet unable to stop this line of talk. Tom lapsed into silence, hunched into his jacket, his face half hidden. Tom said no more either. In another few minutes they were turning into the driveway.

Inside, Tom was detailed to show Michael upstairs and help him unpack. He watched with resentment as Michael tossed his bag on to the spare bed - Duane's bed - and began pulling clothes from it and stuffing them into drawers. He didn't know how he was going to stick a whole weekend with this big-mouth kid and his showing off. As though echoing his thoughts, Michael said, 'I didn't bring many of my things, not just for a weekend. Got lots of other stuff, though. My Mum buys me all the latest gear.'

He stared at Tom, as though daring him to contradict. Tom said wearily, 'That's nice. I think lunch is ready. Let's go down.'

Michael knew that the Kents - at least, Mr and Mrs Kent and Lucy - were working hard at making him feel welcome. They took him to the Science and Wildlife Museum in the afternoon, made pancakes for tea, and in the evening played a card game with him before they all watched a video together. Tom watched for a while, but soon drifted off to the bedroom to play on his computer.

Michael had noticed the small portable TV, the computer and its accessories, all arranged on a trolley in Tom's half of the bedroom. It looked fascinating, and he would have dearly loved a go. Computers and Game Boys were not things they had at Woodcroft Hall. They had been tried, but were fought over and argued about, and soon damaged and broken. In the end, Miss Hall took them away.

Tom didn't offer Michael a turn with his computer games. Michael didn't really blame him - if he'd owned anything like that he would certainly not have let anyone touch it.

Just the same, it would have been good fun. He imagined himself saying to Dean Patterson on Monday morning, 'Tom - that's my new brother - he's got a brand new computer all to himself. He's got all the latest games - *Alien Faces* and *Starship Warrior* and *Supermaze* - all those. Sometimes he makes up new games himself. He's teaching me to make up new games - we spend hours working on it.'

He wished sadly that all this was true.

On Sunday they all went to Church. Michael hadn't been to Church much, but it was nice sitting in a row, he thought, as though they really all belonged together. He peeped sideways at the others, feeling a sense of pride in them all. Mr and Mrs Kent, whom he secretly called Mum and Dad - though he wouldn't have dared to say it to their faces - looked especially smart and nice. He felt proud of Dad when he got up to take round the collection plate, and Mum had a lovely clear singing voice. Lucy looked great, dressed in her latest outfit.

Tom - well, he wasn't quite sure about him. However hard he tried to please - or perhaps because of it - Tom remained distant.

Hunched well down at the end of the row, Tom was feeling more and more uncomfortable as the service went by. Knowing that around him people were praying, Tom remembered how they'd all prayed at home about the fostering business. They'd said thank you to God when Duane had come to live with them. Tom himself had said a very sincere thank you. But then God had taken Duane away again.

Or was it God who had taken him? Mum and Dad said that *all* things worked together for good to those who loved God - and that they were trusting God to send them the right child. They seemed to think that this loud-mouth Michael might be the right child. Well, *he* didn't want Michael, or anyone else - he wanted Duane.

He turned his head a little to look at Michael. Yes, he'd thought so, Michael was squinting at him again, the way he often did, though he pretended not to be when he saw Tom looking. Michael's cheeks went pink, and he looked down, twisting his fingers together. In spite of himself, Tom felt a twinge of pity. It must be tough, having no real home or family, and no one really wanting you. Maybe he'd offer to play football with him after lunch.

But that afternoon the heavens opened and it poured with cold sleety rain. Football was out. Tom considered letting Michael play on the computer. He'd seen him looking longingly at it.

But these good impulses were pushed back by the seed of bitterness he'd allowed to take root inside him. He hardened his heart. Michael spent the afternoon watching another video on TV with Mum and Dad and Lucy, and after tea they drove him back to Woodcroft House.

Chapter Seven

Supermaze

Supermaze was the latest computer game which Tom had recently bought with some money left over from Christmas. The adventure took place in space, through which the player had to find his way through a complicated galactic maze to find his own star-station. Hazards of asteroids and meteors and alien invaders lurked among the scattered stars, all intent on destruction. Michael watched from a distance as Tom manipulated the buttons on the keyboard. It was his eighth weekend with the Kents, and there was talk of his moving in with them before long.

Winter was beginning to melt and merge into early spring. The days were lengthening and forsythia and crocuses bloomed in the gardens. Conditions were improving for outdoor games, and there were Cub Scouts and Youth Club activities in the lighter evenings. Tom still played on his computer, but mostly now at bedtime, in the time they were allowed for reading before lights out.

Tom and Michael now played football together quite a lot. Tom was relieved to find that Michael wasn't quite as good as himself, though he had to admit that he wasn't far behind. It was OK, really, having someone to practise with, without having to go down to the sports centre every time. Michael had mostly given up the tall tales, thank goodness. But Tom still considered him very irritating when he was over-helpful to Mum and Dad, always offering to clean the car or fetch in the washing, behaving like a bit of a creep. It was funny how Mum and Dad couldn't seem to see that he only did it because he was afraid they wouldn't have him any more if he didn't. Still, Michael wasn't quite as bad as he'd feared. There were still some things Tom wasn't prepared to share with him, though. Like the computer games.

Tom negotiated the last part of the space maze, switched off the screen and settled himself for sleep.

''Night, Mike', he said.

'Goodnight,' said Michael, and tossed aside the comic with a small sigh. It would have been nice, just for once, to have his own fingers on the keyboard when that last alien was destroyed.

Next day was Saturday, for Michael now arrived on Friday evenings after school. On Saturday mornings, both boys were expected to share in the cleaning and tidying of their bedroom. But Tom had arranged to be at his friend Adam's house by 10.30 to see his new mountain bike, and he was late.

'I'll do it this afternoon, Mum.'

'We're going on a picnic, as the weather's so lovely,' said Mum. 'Go on, Tom, get it done. You can go to Adam's afterwards.'

'But he'll be off on the bike then.'

'I'll do your share,' offered Michael quickly.

He was rewarded by the look of real gratitude that replaced Tom's frown. 'Thanks, Mike.'

Michael was careful with the vacuum cleaner, hoovering slowly and taking pains not to jog the trolley with its valuable cargo. The computer was still loaded with the *Supermaze* disk.

Switching off the cleaner, Michael hesitated. He had done Tom's Saturday work for him. Surely he deserved one little game with the computer. Tom would never know.

He had watched Tom often enough to learn some tactics, but his responses were nowhere near as fast as Tom's. The first time round he was zapped by an alien very quickly. The third time he got part way through the galaxies. The third time, he was sure he would make it back to the starship.

'What on earth...?'

Tom was standing in the doorway, his face incredulous. Taken by surprise, Michael jumped guiltily from his perch on the side of Tom's bed, giving the trolley a jolt. The TV screen wobbled a little before it steadied. Michael stared apprehensively at Tom.

Tom was furious. He had been too late, after all, to catch Adam and his mountain bike, and his own bike had had a puncture on the way home. To find that creep, Michael, actually having the nerve to meddle with his most prized possession, almost took his breath away. He felt the root of bitterness spring up afresh.

Michael looked the picture of guilt. Fuming, Tom strode across the room and pulled out the television plug. 'You're not to touch that! You're not to touch any of my things! This is my side of the room, and it's private! Don't bother finishing the cleaning. I'm going out!'

He turned and clattered downstairs, and Michael heard the front door open and close with a bang.

Michael's first impulse was to burst into tears. It wasn't fair! He hadn't broken anything or done any harm. He'd only played one or two games. And he'd done all Tom's Saturday work for him. But Tom had never liked him. And now he really hated him.

As he stood on the bedside rug, hands clenched tightly, despair gave way to rage. He had tried his best to please everyone, even to please Tom, but it wasn't any use. Nobody liked him, not really. Well, he didn't care. He hated Tom too - hated all of them.

The keyboard of the little computer and the blank screen seemed to twinkle mockingly at him. He hated Tom's precious computer too. He picked it up from the trolley, wrenched out the plugs connecting the keyboard and flung both to the floor. The sounds of plastic and metal scrunching and buckling mingled with his sobs as he stamped viciously on them again and again.

Chapter Eight

Another Chance

Michael sat on his bed at Woodcroft House. At his feet were two large bulging suitcases, and his sports bag, soccer boots, roller skates and football, all his worldly possessions, were piled beside them. Mike was leaving Woodcroft House, for good.

Dean Patterson drifted in, curious in a cautious way. Michael had grown tougher over the last weeks, and his mood had been unpredictable since his last weekend with the Kents.

'You really going, then?'

Michael nodded glumly.

'For good?'

'Yes.'

'Miss Hall says you're going camping.'

'That's right.'

'Well, you don't look too happy about it. I bet you're not really - not a real camping trip out in the wilds.'

Michael hadn't the spirit to argue. He rose wearily and went into the bathroom across the landing, where he locked the door and sat down dejectedly upon the laundry basket. He thought ironically that for once he could have given Dean a perfectly truthful glowing account of the coming camping trip - out in the real country, by a river, building fires and cooking and perhaps even hunting and fishing for their own food. But he just hadn't the heart.

Michael was confused. He'd been sure that in the act of wrecking Tom's computer he had also wrecked his chances of ever having a home with the Kents - or anyone else, for that matter. It was the episode of the little china bell all over again, or worse, because this time the damage had been deliberate, and because the computer meant so much to Tom. He remembered with a sick feeling the way they'd all looked - Tom horrified and furious, Lucy shocked, Mr and Mrs Kent upset and disappointed. No one had known what to say at first.

'Well, this is a real mess,' said Mr Kent at last, and he hadn't just meant the smashed computer.

They had tried to talk to Michael but he had retreated into silence. Driving him back to Woodcroft House, Mr and Mrs Kent had closeted themselves with Miss Hall, and he was sure that it was the end of everything. He'd had his last chance, and he'd blown it.

Numb despair had turned to sheer disbelief when Miss Hall had called him in later in the week and told him what had been agreed. The Kents had decided it was time for Michael to go to live with them on a permanent basis. He had gasped at Miss Hall, speechless. It was so unexpected. She hadn't even mentioned the smashed computer, though she must have known all about it.

'It's the end of term this week,' said Miss Hall briskly. 'So the Easter holidays seem a good time to get you settled, before the new term begins. Mr Kent is planning on having time off next week to take you and Tom camping. So, when you're packing, don't forget your outdoor stuff.'

Michael's head reeled. He couldn't believe it. They were still taking him on after what had happened. And a special camping trip, almost as though he deserved a reward rather than a punishment? He grew more and more confused as he packed his belongings - all of them, this time. There must be a catch somewhere. People just didn't behave like that after the kind of things he'd done.

It had been a difficult time for the Kents, making up their minds what to do next. Tom had been furious, Lucy almost hysterical, their parents worried and disappointed. There were so many things to be taken into consideration - not least Tom, who had given up his room, his privacy, his time and possessions, and who had perhaps suffered most.

A family discussion was held at the end of a subdued and awkward weekend. Tom was silent. He hated Michael, and felt guilty about hating him, because he had an idea of why Michael had done what he had done. He had sometimes been mean to Michael, especially over the computer, which he knew Michael longed to use. He had an awful feeling that he might have done the same in Michael's place.

But it was awful to see Mum and Dad so upset and so much at a loss. They had tried desperately hard to be fair to both him and Michael. He could see that at first they were so angry on behalf of him, Tom, that they almost wanted to send Michael away for good. But then they'd prayed together, and had said they felt they ought to try again, if the children agreed, because things had been going so well up to now, and because Michael might be damaged even more if they rejected him.

Soft-hearted Lucy was quick to agree. 'I don't think he meant any harm. He just lost his temper. He's nice, usually.'

The three of them looked at Tom.

'What about my computer?' he muttered, head down.

'We've discussed that,' said Dad. 'As you know, Michael has his pocket money from the allowance we're paid for him. We'll make him pay back part of the money for the repair, week by week. I think it can be repaired.'

'What do you think, Tom?' asked Mum gently.

Tom shrugged. 'It's OK with me, I suppose.'

He had a strange feeling, almost of relief. His conscience, he knew, wouldn't have been easy if they'd finished with Michael because of what had happened. He still thought Michael was a creep, and it still made him hopping mad, thinking of him smashing up the computer. But maybe he had been partly to blame.

He raised his head and managed a grin, and repeated, 'It'll be OK, I expect.'

He could see the relief on their faces. Dad reached over and gave his shoulder a punch. 'Good man! I thought perhaps I'd take next week off and we'd go camping, the three of us - maybe in the Golden Valley. What do you think?'

Chapter Nine

Golden Valley Camp

The Golden Valley began as you left the last suburban house behind, opening up ahead as you took the winding country road between fields and woodland, until you reached a point where you could see the valley spread before you with high mountains on one side, gentler sloping farmland on the other, and the silvery, ribbon-like river winding and gliding through the valley on its way to the estuary and eventually, the sea.

Tom and his family picnicked there sometimes in the summer, choosing a nice grassy spot along the river bank, or a place they could climb one of the hills to see the view, or a trip to one of the picturesque little villages along the river. But he had never been camping there before, or camping at all for that matter, unless you counted a little play tent on the front lawn at home, where he and a friend had spent a couple of nights last summer. The thought of real camping, out in the woods or along a river bank, with no houses or shops for miles, filled him with a tingling excitement. As for Michael, who had hardly left town except for organised outings to the zoo or the seaside, the whole expedition had the feel of something from an adventure movie.

That morning, they had loaded the car from boot to roof-rack, with hired camping equipment, gas, supplies, sleeping bags and warm clothing. Lucy was half-envious of the adventure, though too worried about the possibility of spiders, frogs and creepy-crawlies to really want to join them. Besides, there was a new Dance and Drama group beginning at Church which she did not want to miss.

'Drama!' said Tom scornfully 'I'd rather have frogs!'

'Me too,' said Michael. 'Or even toads,' he added, although he wasn't quite sure what a toad looked like.

Michael was still not quite able to believe the latest happenings. The Kents treated him just as they always had, though they had talked to him seriously about having to pay for the computer's repair. Even Tom seemed prepared to try to forget all about it. And there was no catch about the camping trip - they were really going off to the depths of the Golden Valley for a whole week. He couldn't help regretting that he wouldn't be able to brag about it to Dean afterwards. But Woodcroft House was behind him now. He had left there, and he was determined never, never, to go back.

They stopped for sandwiches and coffee at lunchtime, and by mid-afternoon had reached the thickly-wooded part of the valley where Dad planned to make camp. Here willow, ash and alders in bud, clustered to the river bank with its shingly beach, and tall pines bordered the higher bank. Dad had already obtained permission to camp, and he drove the loaded car carefully along a bumpy track and stopped at a flat, grassy space, perfect for camping.

Tom jumped out of the car and rushed at once to the river's edge to peer into the clear, brownish-green water bubbling over grey-brown stones.

'Fish!' he yelled in delight. 'Dad, there are fish! Come and look!'

His father came crunching over the stony shingle to stand beside him. 'Trout,' he said. 'The river was polluted, and nothing's been able to live in it for the past few years, but it's cleared. And the trout are back!'

'We could catch some and cook them for our meals,' said Tom eagerly. 'Could we make a real fire and do proper cooking, Dad, instead of just using the stove?'

His father laughed. 'We could try it one of these nights, if you like, but after a couple of meals of charred bacon and raw sausages, you might be glad to get back to the stove.'

Watching the two of them, father and son, Michael felt a little out of things. They so obviously belonged together, while he - well, he wasn't quite sure where he fitted in. Or if he fitted at all. When the social workers had talked about finding a family for him, he'd imagined that he'd almost immediately be part of the family, an instant son to the parents and brother to the children. It hadn't worked out like that, not with the Merediths, not even with the Kents, partly his own fault, but not altogether.

Would they ever really accept him, he wondered, staring a little wistfully at the smooth brown fish among the stones in the clear water. Was there anything more he could do that would make them accept him?

An idea came to him later in the evening. They had unpacked the camping gear, pitched the two green nylon tents, organised the stove and gas cylinder and filled the water container with fresh water from a spring higher up the bank. They'd boiled water for tea, heated baked beans, and fried bacon and eggs on the stove, washed up in river water heated in a pan, laid out the sleeping bags for turning in later, and gone for a walk along the river bank.

It was a beautiful April evening. Budding vegetation sprouted new growth along the bank and violets and primroses peeped out from shaded spots. A soft new film of tender green covered the trees and bushes, and small birds nested and twittered in the branches. Fresh new grass grew in the water meadow, and sheep had been turned in to graze it. Most of them had new lambs, with springy legs and shrill voices.

'This is the life!' said Dad. 'Beats toiling away in an office any time.'

Tom, true to form, had already fallen out of a willow tree, scraping his knee on the way down, and had got two pairs of socks soaked wading in water over the tops of his Wellington boots. The second time he had lost his balance and sat down in the water up to his armpits, laughing and spluttering. Dad got him a dry change of clothes and said that he'd frighten away all the fish if he carried on like that.

The more cautious Michael was careful to keep his feet dry and his knees unscathed. Years of looking out for his own interests had taught him to avoid trouble of any kind whenever possible. He secretly rather envied Tom with his daring attitude, though he was sometimes rather shocked at the risks Tom took. He'd surely break an arm or a leg, at least, if he carried on like this for the whole week.

And that was when the thought came. Sooner or later, out here in the wilds, Tom was sure to put himself in a position of real danger. If he, Michael, watched for his chance and managed to rescue Tom, then surely the past would be forgiven and forgotten. He daydreamed pleasantly about Tom saying, 'You saved my life! Now we're really brothers!'

That kind of thing happened in films. It would solve all the problems in one go.

Michael was so cheered by this idea that he joined Tom in a wet and splashy washing session at the water's edge, during which he got one of his own boots half full of water. Squelching and giggling, they returned to the camp where Dad had rigged up the light and was boiling water for cocoa.

Chapter Ten

Golden Valley Night

In the Kent's home, Mum and Dad always had short prayers and a Bible reading with the children before they went to bed. Michael had grown used to this, though he always partly switched off when it was going on. He often wondered whether it was meant for him too, though he'd been surprised to find that Mum or Dad prayed for him by name too, as well as for Lucy and Tom.

He didn't expect that Dad would carry on with this kind of thing while they were at camp. So it was a surprise when Dad produced his Bible with the worn leather cover, while they were all sipping hot cocoa together in the boys' tent. Instead of reading a piece straight off, Dad said, 'When I was a little boy, my dad used to read me stories, sometimes from a set of encyclopaedias called *Tales the Woodman Told*. They were kind of parables, all about wild life, told by an old American hunter and trapper to his young grandson. I loved them. I wondered whether, other nights when we've got a fire going, you'd like us to do something like that.'

Both boys looked at him expectantly. It sounded more fun than the usual routine.

'Are you going to make them up yourself?' asked Tom.

'I'll try,' said Dad with a grin. 'It'll be good for me. They won't be half as good as the Woodman's, but then I'm not an American hunter.'

'Well, go on, then,' said Tom, settling the sleeping bag more comfortably about himself. 'That is, if you've made one up already.'

'A very simple one. The river gave me the idea,' said Dad. 'Once upon a time, there was a beautiful river, clear as crystal, sparkling in the sun, winding its way through a lovely valley, watering the cattle and crops. It was so clear that millions of fish lived in it, children swam and paddled along its edges, and it was even perfectly safe to drink from. Then something began to happen. People began to allow waste from factories, and detergents and household waste water to seep into the river, not much at first, but increasing as more people came along and more factories were built. The river began to be dirty, and scum formed on its surface. Then the water plants couldn't grow, and the fish began to die. People dared not swim or paddle, and animals couldn't drink, because the water was polluted. The whole river stank.'

The boys listened, Michael sleepy but interested.

'But it's clean again now. How did that happen?' asked Tom.

'Well,' said Dad. 'Some people realised how terrible it was that the river was being destroyed. They decided it must stop. They stopped pouring waste into the river, and disposed of rubbish elsewhere. That improved things a little, but didn't really solve the problem. Then someone invented a chemical which, when poured into the water, restored the right balance. Weeds and plants began to grow again, fish came back and the water sparkled again. Soon, it was even clean enough for boys to wash in.'

Michael thought that was the end of the story. But there was more.

'I thought,' said Dad, 'that in the beginning the river was like people the way God first made them, all pure and new. Then sin came in when Adam disobeyed God, and everyone became kind of dirty and polluted because of it. No matter how much the human race tried to clean itself up, it could never succeed. Until God sent the right kind of chemical to do the trick.'

Michael was puzzled. Did the Bible really talk about God using chemicals?

'The chemical of the blood of Jesus,' said Dad. 'When Jesus died, he took the punishment for everyone's sin. When the chemical of his blood is put into our lives, it makes us perfectly clean.' He read from his Bible some verses which said, 'The blood of Jesus Christ makes us clean from all sin.'

Both boys were silent. Tom admired Dad's story very much, though the moral part of it made him feel quite uncomfortable. As a little boy he'd loved Jesus, but just lately, he didn't know why, he was a bit confused about God. He still blamed God for taking Duane away, whenever he thought about it. Dad thought you could trust God in everything, but he wasn't so sure. Anyway, he'd put it out of his mind. That was what he did with things he didn't want to think about.

'That was a great story, Dad,' he said, 'Try a bit harder, and I might give you an "A" for the next one.'

Dad grinned, then he tucked up both boys in their sleeping bags. He said a brief prayer in which he mentioned Mum and Lucy at home.

Michael lay awake for a time in the darkened tent, listening through the thin canvas walls to the sounds of Dad pottering about tidying up, and then going into his own tent. The light was out and it was quite dark now. There was the sound of Tom's soft breathing, the faint babbling of the river and the hoot of an owl from the bushes along the bank.

He had only half understood the story about the polluted river and the chemical that made it clean. It was odd how Jesus seemed so real to some people, like Mum and Dad Kent, and Carol. To Michael, he was just someone in a story, shadowy and vague. He hadn't a clue whether it was all true or not. Yet, he suddenly remembered he had asked God to help him that time, after leaving the Merediths, and not long after, he'd come to the Kents. And the Kents had kept him on, even after he'd smashed the computer. Could God have had something to do with it?

Anyway, he was sleepy, in spite of the unfamiliar hardness of the ground under the thin foam mattress. He yawned and turned over, moving the pillow into a more comfortable position.

Michael was dreaming. In the dream, he was trying to rescue Tom from the jaws of some strange alien with large teeth and a shrill, squeaky kind of voice. He awoke in a fright, forgetting for a moment where he was, then realising with relief that he was in a tent and dreaming.

But was it a dream? The shrill, squeaking frightened voice was there, somewhere outside, and next moment there was a thump and a scuffle as something cannoned into the green nylon wall.

Chapter Eleven

Lost Lamb

Tom awoke as Michael struggled to free himself from the sleeping bag.

'What's going on? What's that noise?'

Michael's heart was thumping with terror. Something was there, outside the tent, trying to get in. He tried to speak but his mouth was dry with fear.

Tom scrambled from the tent opening, almost bumping into Dad, who was emerging from his own tent with a torch.

'It's okay. Just a lamb. It's got itself mixed up with the tent ropes.'

The torch beam showed a small lamb with a black nose, trying to butt itself into the tent wall in panic, and bleating in a high, shrill voice. Dad caught it and calmed its struggles.

'It belongs to one of those ewes in the meadow, I expect,' said Dad. 'It's wandered away. I wonder where its mum is?'

He shone the torch in a wide circle, but there was no sign or sound of any other sheep.

'What shall we do with it?' asked Tom.

Dad looked at his watch. 'It's not four o'clock yet. I'll put it in the trailer for now. It won't starve before morning. Then if its mum hasn't appeared, we'll take it up to the farm. All right, Michael?'

'Yes, thanks.' Michael was feeling a little ashamed of being so frightened by nothing more sinister than a little lost lamb. And to think he'd been dreaming of saving Tom's life! He crawled out, glad of the darkness, and watched Dad put the lamb into the trailer and cover it with a tarpaulin. It bleated forlornly for a while and then lay down in a corner.

After their disturbed night everyone overslept. While Dad cooked breakfast, the boys tried to get the lamb to drink some milk, but it wouldn't lap like a cat or dog, and a proper feeding bottle wasn't part of their camping equipment. It was hungry by now, and its shrill cries rang in their ears as they ate their own breakfast. None of the other sheep were to be seen.

Dad consulted his large-scale map to see where the farmhouse and buildings were. 'Up the bank, through the gate, across the next field, and you should see the farmhouse over the brow of the next hill,' he said. 'Can you boys manage to take the lamb back yourselves while I clear up here?'

They said that they could. They set off with Tom carrying the lamb. For such a small creature it was surprisingly heavy and it wriggled continuously, still crying for its mother, and he was glad to let Michael take a turn. Both boys were warm and flushed by the time they came in sight of the white-walled farmhouse, surrounded by grey stone buildings.

They were greeted by a black-and-white sheepdog, barking and wagging its tail at the same time. The farmer was in the stock yard, feeding silage to his cattle with a tractor and fork lift, a stocky middle-aged man who seemed surprised to see the two boys and the lamb. He stopped the tractor and listened to their explanation.

'Yes, that looks like one of mine. Wonder where its mother got to? Can you wait a minute while I finish this, and then we'll go and look, if you'd like to come along. Put him in that pen at the end, for a minute, and rest your arms.'

Tom carried the lamb over to the pen. The farmer leaned on his steering wheel, looking down at Michael. 'You the people that are camping down by the river, by any chance?'

When Michael nodded he went on, 'Must be your Dad I spoke to then, when he phoned to make the arrangements.'

Tom was out of earshot for the moment. Michael felt his cheeks grow flushed. 'Yes,' he said. 'My Dad's taking us camping for the whole week. Just the three of us. Dad, and me and my - my brother.' He would have said more, warming to the subject, but Tom was coming back across the yard.

They waited, admiring the huge machines in one of the buildings while the farmer finished feeding his cattle. Then he fetched a long shepherd's crook, whistled for the sheepdog, picked up the lamb, and headed for the river meadows with the two boys.

It was going to be another glorious day when the small chilly curls of early mist from the river had dispersed. Breasting the hill they saw their camp, tents darker green against the light green grass, and the small figure of Dad pottering about the camp. The sheep had scattered and were grazing, white dots on the meadow, the picture of tranquillity. None of them seemed to be missing the hungry little lamb in the farmer's arms.

'There's always some that'll wander off, but mostly the ewes keep track of them,' he said as they set off down the hill.

It was the dog who found the missing ewe as he nosed about in the undergrowth far ahead of the other searchers. She was caught up in a bramble bush, almost exhausted from her struggles and hoarse with bleating for her lost lamb. The farmer put down the lamb and worked to release her, leaving handfuls of her wool behind in the bush. Tired as she was, as soon as she was free, the ewe rushed to her lamb, bleating endearments and nosing anxiously at it. The lamb at once began to suckle, butting its mother with a hard round head and wriggling its tail in delirious joy. The farmer patted his dog and looked at mother and child with satisfaction.

'Thanks very much, lads. I check the sheep over every day, but I might have missed this one if you hadn't brought the lamb. I'm much obliged. By the way, if your Dad wants to buy eggs or milk or vegetables, we sell them all at the farm.'

They were turning towards the camp when he called them back, digging about in the pockets of his boiler suit. 'Just a minute. Here's something for you.'

He brought out two rather battered-looking Mars Bars, which he handed to Tom.

'One for you, and one for your brother. And thanks very much.'

'We're not brothers,' said Tom quickly. 'And thank *you* very much.'

The farmer glanced briefly at Michael, but only said, 'Cheerio!' before striding off, the dog at his heels. Tom and Michael wandered along the river bank towards the camp, munching the Mars Bars which tasted very faintly of diesel oil. Why had Tom had to go and say that, thought Michael, resentfully. He'd been enjoying the morning so far, and that remark had gone and spoilt it.

Even the sun had gone behind a cloud.

Chapter Twelve

Left Alone

'There's a change coming in the weather,' said the farmer next morning.

They had discovered that the farmer's name was Mr Whitely. Dad had sent them over to the farm to buy fresh milk, eggs and potatoes.

The boys gazed at the sky, which to them seemed as blue and clear as ever. 'Is there?' asked Tom.

The farmer nodded, pushing back his cap and scratching his head. 'Yes. I've just listened to the forecast. Rain - maybe heavy rain, and some wind with it. Better tell your dad to make sure those tents of yours are secure and watertight. You don't want them blown away.'

'I'll tell him,' said Tom. They said goodbye to Mr Whitely and set off up the hill, studying the sky at intervals. At first glance it looked innocent enough, but when you really took notice there was a steely tinge to the blueness that hadn't been there before. The breeze felt chilly, too. They reported to Dad what the farmer had said.

'I missed the forecast,' said Dad. 'But it does look rather like rain. Well, the tents are good and secure, and we've got plenty of waterproofs. We should be okay. We don't want to pack up and go home because of a shower or two, do we?'

Both boys agreed. Tom secretly hoped they were in for a good storm, with thunder and lightning perhaps. It would be fun to lie snugly in the sleeping bags and watch lightning flash along the river bank and hear rain drumming on taut canvas.

Michael didn't think about thunder and lightning, but he too had no wish to pack up and go home yet. In spite of everything he was enjoying the trip. He and Tom had rigged up fishing lines baited with scraps of bacon rind, and had managed to catch a fish each. Michael's was rather small, but it was the first fish he had ever caught. They had cooked them for supper and pronounced them delicious, though both privately noticing the rather smoky and muddy flavour.

In the afternoon, Dad had shown them how to make a proper camp fire, carefully digging out turfs and putting them to one side to be neatly replaced later. He had built the fire with dry twigs underneath to kindle quickly, with larger dead branches from along the banks to keep it going. When it was lit at dusk it had made quite a blaze, lighting up the camp and the trees around it, giving a ruddy tinge to the river water and to their hands and faces. The smell of wood smoke was pleasant, though they found it clung stubbornly to their hands and hair and clothes afterwards. Sitting around the fire, Dad had told them another modern parable.

'That lost lamb gave me the idea for this one,' he said. 'Once upon a time, a lamb lived with its mum and other sheep in a lovely grassy meadow with a stream running through. All day long he ran and played with the other lambs and nibbled sweet grass. The shepherd took good care of them. But this lamb wasn't content. Every day he looked through the hedge at the woods beyond and wished he could go there instead. The grass seemed greener, the trees shady and the woods more exciting. His mother told him over and over that the woods were not safe because of the wild animals that lurked there. But he tossed his head and wouldn't listen.

'One day, the lamb found a small hole in the hedge. Quickly he squeezed through and darted down a little winding path into the wood. It was very pleasant there. He kicked up his heels, trotted here and there, nibbling fresh new grass. Much better than the boring old field. He spent a lovely afternoon. Then it was time to go home before night came. The lamb looked for the pathway, but couldn't remember which it was. Lots of paths criss-crossed each other and all looked alike. He searched until he was tired out. Then he stopped. He was lost.

It was quite dark. Strange noises came from the woods, rustlings and gruntings. Wild animals were about. Suddenly there was a loud crashing sound. The lamb jumped up and ran. But the ground gave way under him. He fell, down, down into a deep pit.

'There was no way out. The lamb cried and cried, in the bottom of the pit. He wished he'd never, never, disobeyed.

'Then, suddenly, he heard a voice. It was a familiar one. It was the shepherd's voice. He had his lantern and his long crook. Quickly he called to his lamb, telling him he was found. Then he hauled him out of the horrible pit and carried him safely home in his arms.'

Dad paused. The two boys looked at him expectantly. They knew that Dad would have a bit more to add to the story.

'I think you know that Jesus is the Good Shepherd,' he said. 'Always searching for the lost ones, that wander away from him to do their own thing. Never giving up on them. Always happy when He's found them at last.'

That was all he said. But both boys went to sleep thinking of the Good Shepherd who never gave up searching for His lost sheep.

Next day they had explored, following the river upstream, discovering little inlets, a bridge, and even a tiny island, covered with trees, in the middle of the river. Tom badly wanted to make a boat to try to row to the island, but Dad said a definite 'no' to that.

'The water's deep just there - you wouldn't be safe. Yes, I know you can swim, but not strongly enough to swim against a current. Promise you won't try anything like that, Tom.'

Tom reluctantly promised. Michael had by now given up the idea of trying to save Tom's life. Tom, though accident-prone and given to taking risks, seemed more than capable of looking after himself. When they had almost trodden on what Michael thought was a snake, it was Michael who turned pale and shaky, and Tom who laughed, said it was a slow-worm, and picked it up on a stick to put it out of harm's way.

That night, Dad's story had been another one based on sheep. While the boys fished, Dad had gone to the farm and given Mr Whitely a hand with the ewes and lambs. Mr Whitely had pointed out one particular ewe, who having lost her own lamb at birth, had been given a triplet lamb from another ewe with not enough milk to feed three. 'That lamb was adopted by a new mother,' said Dad, and went on to say that there were lots of places in the Bible that talked about adoption. 'In fact, I'm an adopted child myself,' said Dad.

Both boys looked at him, startled. 'Are you really, Dad?' asked Tom.

'Yes,' said Dad. 'In a way. God adopted me into his family when I accepted Jesus, and that means I'm a true son of God, with all the privileges that he gave to his real son, Jesus.'

Michael had grown silent at the mention of adoption. Adoption into a family was what everyone without parents longed for at Woodcroft House. Did all this talk of adoption mean that Dad was thinking of adopting him into the family? He dared not really believe this might happen, but he allowed himself a tiny spark of hope.

'We're getting low on a few supplies,' said Dad, as they finished breakfast. 'I think I'll drive into the village to stock up, and to post our cards to Mum and Lucy. Are you two coming?'

The thought of civilisation, with shops and houses and traffic, seemed deadly dull to Tom. He wondered how he had ever managed to survive that kind of life before camp, with the added hassle of clean clothes and showers and school.

'I'll stay,' he said.

'I'll stay too,' said Michael quickly, though he wasn't sure how he'd feel without Dad or any other grown-up about.'

'Right,' said Dad. 'A bit of independence might do you both good. I won't be long. I think I can trust you to stay out of the river. And you might as well make your-selves useful and do the washing up.'

He made a list of things they needed, checked the gas and petrol, climbed into the car, and bumped away up the track to the road.

The first drops of rain began to fall while Tom and Michael were finishing the last of the washing up. They hurried to stow everything into Dad's tent, and to cover what couldn't be moved. The rain kept on, not heavy but enough to set the trees and vegetation dripping, and to make the ground around the camp begin to be muddy. Tom and Michael put on their anoraks and Wellingtons and waited for Dad to come back.

Michael was worried and even Tom seemed a little anxious when Dad still hadn't returned at mid-day. The rain had grown heavier and they retreated to their own tent, lunching on bread and cheese and the last of the milk. They did not attempt to light the stove for boiling tea.

'I thought Dad would be back for lunch,' said Tom.

'What he said was, he wouldn't be long,' said the more precise Michael.

'But how long is not long?' wondered Tom.

Michael didn't know. But it was beginning to seem very long.

Both were anxious about Dad though neither would admit it. Tom found a pile of comics among his things, and though they were ones they'd both seen before, they settled down on the sleeping bags to read the more exciting bits again.

Chapter Thirteen

Wet Weather

'Do you think he forgot the time?'

''Course not.'

'Well, do you think the car broke down?'

'No. It's just been MOT'd.'

'Do you think he went home or something? Just for a visit?'

Tom rustled his magazine crossly. 'Don't be daft! And shut up. I'm trying to read.' He pretended to be absorbed in a futuristic strip cartoon, but Michael knew he wasn't really seeing it at all.

Michael felt his own lip wobble. Rain drummed steadily on the tent walls. The wind was rising, and the budding willows on the river bank made a sighing sound. There was another noise too, a slight snuffling and padding.

'Tom...'

'I said, shut up! If you're scared, you shouldn't have come camping.'

'But there's something outside...'

Tom threw down the comic in exasperation. He glared across at Michael. But next moment, a black and white face with a long pointed nose peered enquiringly round the tent opening. A shaggy body and long tail, waving gently, followed.

'It's Mr Whitely's dog, from the farm,' said Tom. 'Spot.'

It was amazing how much better they felt for seeing the dog. Spot shook his wet coat all over Michael's sleeping bag. Michael tried to fend him off, while Tom dragged on his boots and scrambled outside. Mr Whitely himself was coming down the hill, squelching through the rain and mud in a long waterproof coat and Wellingtons. He called out when he was within earshot.

'A message for you two. Your father just phoned.'

Michael joined Tom at the tent doorway. They waited for the message.

'I'm afraid he's had a bit of an accident. Don't worry - not serious.'

'What kind of accident?'

'Bit of a bump in the car. Someone ran into him from behind. Nothing serious, like I said. But your Dad's had a bang on the head and they took him to the cottage hospital. Seems he was knocked out for a short while. No bones broken, but they want him to stay in overnight, for observation. They always do that after a knock on the head.

'You're sure he's all right?' Michael thought that Tom sounded upset.

Mr Whitely squeezed his shoulder with a wet hand. Water dripped from the brim of the sou'wester hat he wore. 'He's fine. You're not to worry. He's anxious about you two, though. Asked if I'd come down and take you back to the farmhouse overnight, if you'd like to come.'

Michael and Tom looked at one another. Michael could see that a mighty load had lifted from Tom's shoulders with knowing about Dad. He felt dizzy with relief himself. They'd be dry and cosy at the farm overnight, and tomorrow Dad would be back.

'You'd be no trouble,' said Mr Whitely, as Tom hesitated. 'My missus'd be pleased to have you. And she's a real good cook.'

'Thanks a lot,' said Tom. 'But I think we can manage. We'll be fine. Won't we Michael?'

Michael's stomach did a strange kind of flip. Did Tom really mean to stay all night in the camp, in the rain, quite alone? He gulped and nodded dumbly.

Mr Whitely had a doubtful look. 'Are you quite sure, now. Have you camped out alone before?'

Tom nodded. 'Oh yes. Last year. I camped out with a friend of mine, all by ourselves.'

He didn't mention that it had only been two nights on his own lawn in the middle of summer, with Mum and Dad and home just a stone's throw away.

Mr Whitely rubbed his chin. 'Well, I s'pose it's all right as long as you've done it before. Don't forget now, we're just over the hill, the missus and me. If you change your minds, or get in any kind of fix, just come on over.'

'Thank you.'

'Well, I'll say good afternoon then. I'd get out of those damp clothes if I was you. Don't want to catch your deaths of cold.'

He whistled to the dog and strode away, making a detour to see the sheep and lambs, huddling for shelter under the dripping trees and bushes.

Michael looked apprehensively at Tom. Tom looked defiantly at Michael. 'That's that, then. Ought to be good fun, spending the night here on our own. Not scared, are you?'

Michael shook his head. But he couldn't help a small shiver. It would be dark before long. And they'd be here alone on the river bank, when they could have been safe at the farm.

'Better get changed, like Mr Whitely said,' said Tom briskly. 'Wait a bit though - we ought to do the outside work first and *then* get changed. No point in getting two lots of clothes wet. We'd better get something to eat from Dad's tent.'

They found a tin of corned beef, tomatoes and bread and butter, and a carton of fruit juice. Tom looked longingly at the stove but didn't quite have the nerve to try and get it going himself. It was too wet to light a fire. Rather silently, they found dry things to change into and ate their makeshift meal inside the tent.

Dusk was falling and a sharp wind was blowing the rain in spattering gusts against the nylon tent walls.

'I wonder if it'll rain all night,' said Michael uneasily.

They would have liked to listen to the weather forecast, but found that the small radio had gone with Dad.

'It might. I think the wind's getting stronger too,' said Tom.

They turned in early, as there wasn't much else they could do. Both of them were quieter than usual as they undressed and crawled into their sleeping bags. Michael lay awake, listening to the sounds of rain and wind. The tent was watertight, and not even a drop came in. But it was scary, knowing they were all alone on a dark muddy river bank.

'Tom?' whispered Michael after a while.

'Yes?'

'Are you awake?'

'Well, I am now. What's the matter?'

'I was just thinking. We never said any prayers. Do

you think we ought to? Your dad always does.'

'Oh, yes. I forgot. All right then. Er - I'll start.'

Michael heard him mutter a quick prayer. He muttered the Lord's Prayer himself. Somehow it didn't seem at all like when Dad was there, explaining things and talking confidently to God, as though he was right there in the tent with them.

After the prayers, Tom tossed and turned. He'd been almost asleep and that creep Michael had woken him up. The ground felt hard and uncomfortable. He knew Michael was scared. Tom had thought it might be fun, spending the night alone - with himself, of course, in charge. But it wasn't all that much. There were none of the usual friendly sounds of lambs bleating and owls hooting, just the rain and wind and the river, which he was sure was roaring louder than usual. There was another sound too - a little sniffy, muffled gulp. Michael was crying.

Suddenly, Tom was sorry he'd been mean.

'Are you all right, Mike?' he whispered into the darkness.

The unexpected kindness in his voice made Michael sob in earnest.

'I - I'm a bit scared.'

'Don't worry,' said Tom, no longer sounding scornful at all. 'It's not all that much fun without Dad, is it? Tell you the truth, I'm a bit scared myself.'

Michael stopped sniffing in sheer surprise. He gulped down a rising sob, and said, 'It's... it's just the wind, and the dark...'

'And the rain, and Dad not being here,' said Tom.

'Yes.'

They lay in sympathetic silence for a moment listening

to the river's roar and the rain lashing the tent.

Then Michael said in a small voice, 'Tom, it... it might help a bit if we moved the sleeping bags a bit closer together.'

He half expected Tom to be scornful again. But to his relief, Tom said, 'That's a good idea. I ought to have thought of that myself. Let's move.'

They shuffled and wriggled inside their sleeping bags until they were lying side by side, just touching. Tom was surprised to find what a comfort it was to hear Michael's breathing and to know that he was close.

Michael had stopped sniffing, too, thank goodness.

'Tom?'

'Yes?'

'Do you really believe God hears us when we pray?'

Tom considered. He was surprised to find that the hard bitter feelings of hurt and resentment seemed to have faded away and gone. 'Yes, I do,' he said, and really meant it.

'Then can we pray again, and ask him to take care of us?'

'If you like.'

They were silent for a while after their second round of prayers. Tom was drifting towards sleep.

'Tom?'

'Yes?'

'I'm really sorry I smashed up your computer.'

All of a sudden, Tom wondered why he'd thought so much of that computer. He'd hardly missed it at all these last few days. Maybe he was growing out of computer games.

'That's all right. I was mean, too, not letting you use

it. You can play on it when it's mended, if you like.'

'Thanks.'

In spite of the beating rain and roaring water, they were both asleep in five minutes.

Chapter Fourteen

River in Flood

It was still dark when Tom was wakened by something thudding against the tent, near the entrance. He reached for the torch and crawled out of the sleeping bag.

The torch beam showed quite a large branch, with budding leaves and catkins, which had blown down from a willow and been hurled against the tent, where it was entangled with the ropes.

If anything, the storm had worsened. Tom dislodged the branch and investigated, with a waterproof flung over his pyjamas and his boots pulled hastily on. Rain was still teeming down, and the torch beam showed the trees along the bank wildly tossing their branches in the wind, with leaves and bits of twig flying from them.

When Tom turned the torch towards the river, he got a shock. The water was roaring angrily, muddy and dark with white scum forming where it touched the bank, with more branches and twigs floating and whirling downstream. It had risen several inches since the rain began. To Tom's horror, he saw that in the lowest places, the water was already over the tops of the banks and advancing up the meadow.

The river was in flood. It was still some distance from the tents, but Tom knew that if the rain kept coming, the water might soon reach them and they would be flooded. It wasn't safe to wait until the morning.

He ducked back into the tent. 'Michael! Wake up!'

Michael woke confused, taking a moment to come to his senses. 'What? What's happened?'

'The river's flooding. It's creeping up the bank already. We'll have to move.'

Michael scrambled out of the sleeping bag in a panic, ready to take flight just as he was, barefoot and in pyjamas.

'Put some clothes on, and your Wellingtons,' said Tom. 'The water's miles away yet - well, feet, anyway. But hurry up.'

He found his own sweater and jeans and pulled them on over his pyjamas.

'What about the tents and all the stuff?' asked Michael suddenly.

Tom stopped in the middle of zipping his anorak. He hadn't thought of the camping equipment, which was hired, and which Dad would have to pay for, if it got lost or damaged.

'We'll have to take down the tent and move everything up the bank, up under the trees on the high ground,' he decided. 'The water won't come that high. We'll go to the farm then and wait for Dad.'

It was very difficult trying to dismantle tents when the wind was whipping the wet nylon, the rain was stinging your eyes and the only light was the feeble beam of a couple of torches. Both boys' hands were wet, cold and numb by the time they had pulled up the pegs and collapsed the tents in a heap. They heaved the wet material and dangling ropes up the bank and left them there weighed down with two large stones to stop them blowing away. Then they quickly fetched their sleeping bags and belongings before they blew away too.

'Everything's sopping already,' panted Tom, finding more stones to anchor everything. 'But it'll dry out. Better than letting it all get swept away down the river.'

The water was advancing by the time they returned for the last load, creeping up the muddy grass in ominous little swirls and eddies. The river roared on, dark and menacing beyond. The pleasant sunny camp of the last few days was gone, leaving a morass of mud and darkness and threatening water. The boys were wet and cold and tired, fumbling with the cooking stove, Dad's belongings and all the other odds and ends of a camp. Between them they lugged and tugged the gas cylinder up the bank, slipping and sliding in the mud. Checking for anything left behind, Tom was horrified to see the large plastic water container, caught by the latest swirl of water, go bobbing out into midstream. It quickly disappeared downstream, tugged by an unseen current.

'Well, it's the only thing we lost. We got everything else,' he said.

Michael was silent, bedraggled and dripping, his heart thumping painfully. It made him shudder to think of what might have happened if they hadn't discovered the rising water. Maybe he and Tom would have been swept downstream, sleeping bags and all, like that water container.

The first grey streaks of a stormy dawn were beginning to show in the sky. Wearily they climbed the bank to the wet pile of camping equipment. They covered it as best they could with groundsheets, and rested for a moment, leaning against a large ash trunk. The storm raged on, lashing the trees and bushes, sending rain stinging into their numb faces.

'It's nearly morning,' said Tom. 'Come on, let's get moving. The stuff will be safe there - we'll get it later when Dad comes.'

They began wearily to climb through the belt of trees and bushes that fringed the river bank. It was wet and slippery, the wind was against them, they were cold, wet and tired. Michael felt a strong desire to burst into tears. But he fought it down. If Tom could manage to stay cheerful, then so could he.

The wind was still very strong. An extra powerful gust brought them almost to a standstill, catching their breaths. The trees bent and swayed in a frantic dance. Above the noise of the wind came a new sound, an ominous, ripping, tearing, wrenching groan of agony. A large dead elm tree had given up the struggle to stay upright and had come crashing to the ground just ahead, torn up by its roots.

Chapter Fifteen

Rescues

They were in the path of the great dead tree. Michael slithered over sideways, the dry twiggy ends of the nearest branches just whipping his face. He gathered himself up at once, shocked and terrified by the suddenness of the crash. Tom was nowhere to be seen. The great tree lay on its side among the undergrowth, its roots torn out and exposed in the stormy dawn.

'Tom!' cried Michael in terror.

A weak voice answered from somewhere amongst the tangle of branches. 'I'm here.'

Michael's heart flipped in relief. For a moment he'd been sure that Tom had been killed, lying dead and crushed under the great trunk. He slithered down and began to fumble frantically among the dead twiggy branches.

'I'm here,' repeated Tom faintly. 'But my leg's stuck.'

His left leg was caught under a branch, pinning him to the muddy ground. Michael saw his white face looking up through a mass of twigs. 'Is it... is it broken?' he quavered.

'No, I can wiggle my toes all right. But it hurts and I can't get out. You'll have to get help.'

Tom's voice was quavery, too, and Michael could tell that he was trying hard not to cry. He began to part the branches, breaking off twigs that got in the way, so that he could get close to Tom.

'I'll try and get you out,' he said.

The rain was beginning to slacken a little at last, and the sky was growing lighter. Michael could see the branch across Tom's left leg, and his heart sank. It was dead, like the rest of the elm, but solid and thick. He knew he'd never be able to move it or break it. He squatted down beside Tom.

'I can't move the branch - it's too big. I'll have to try and dig underneath your leg.'

'There's the spade,' said Tom. 'From the camping stuff.'

The leg was hurting quite badly and he had a feeling of panic. It was an awful feeling, being pinned down and trapped with your face against the muddy ground. He was glad Michael was there, that he was not alone.

Michael was quickly back with the spade, with which he scraped away at the earth and leaf-mould under and around Tom. The tree's twigs got in the way and poked him in the face, but he persevered. He was rewarded when Tom said, 'I think I can move a bit now. Perhaps I could wriggle out of my boot and get my leg out.'

Michael tossed aside the spade and dug with his hands in the dirt, scooping out a shallow trench around the trapped leg. Then, with Tom heaving with his arms and Michael tugging at Tom's shoulders, they gradually pulled him free, leaving his boot behind under the branch. They collapsed in a heap, muddy and panting, and rested for a moment. Then Michael rescued the boot while Tom investigated the damage to his leg. There was a long scrape on the shin where the branch had caught it, with a large bruise beginning to discolour the skin around it, but nothing seemed to be broken. On being helped up, Tom found that the leg would take his weight and that he could walk, though he felt a little sick and shaky.

The boys looked at each other, soaked, battered and bruised. 'Thanks, Mike,' said Tom, and pulled on his boot. It was almost light. A new day was beginning. A little flicker of excitement rose inside him. This was a real adventure, better than any computer games. What a tale they'd have to tell Dad.

They turned their faces towards the farm again. At the brow of the hill, they turned for a last view of the flooded river. Both boys gasped. Where their camp had been, water now flowed, covering grass and undergrowth in a wide sheet of angry water. The river looked twice its usual width. Bits of branch, twigs, and leaves floated with it, torn off and tossed into the flood.

'Wow!' said Tom in an awed voice.

Michael said nothing. They'd almost been caught in that, he and Tom, caught and swept away in that dark raging torrent. He shivered, and then gasped. Most of the sheep were far up the bank, huddled well away from the water level, their lambs about them. But one ewe was bleating frantically at the water's edge, running back and fore in agitation. Michael could see why. Her lamb was trapped, standing on a little knoll of grass that stuck out of the swirling water, marooned on its own small island.

He caught Tom's arm and pointed. 'Look! It's trapped. It can't reach its mother, and she can't reach it.'

'We'll tell Mr Whitely,' said Tom. Then he stopped. What if that lamb tried to swim? Could it? What if it fell into the water and was swept away? What if the mother tried to reach it and was swept away too?

He turned, limping a little on the injured leg. 'Mike,

we've got to go and get it. We can't just leave it like that.'

'No,' said Michael. 'We can't.' He yawned, thinking longingly of the warm farm kitchen, a hot drink, food, rest. But they'd have to wait. Wearily he followed Tom, plodding and sliding back down the muddy hill towards the flooded water meadow.

Chapter Sixteen

Holding On

At the farm, the Whitelys had slept somewhat uneasily. Mr Whitely, his wife and his son, Ben, had all been aware that a rough night was ahead. Mrs Whitely, in particular, had been anxious. 'Those poor lambs, out all alone on that river bank,' she fretted as darkness fell, and she didn't mean the sheep.

'They seemed determined to stick it out,' said her husband. 'Sensible lads they seem, used to camping. They'll be all right.'

But he, too, was uneasy, though he was not quite sure why. The boys had enough sense to stay away from the river. They'd be tucked up snug in their sleeping bags by now, and be as pleased as punch tomorrow to tell their dad how they'd stuck it out all by themselves. The thought of flooding never entered his head. The sheep always grazed the water meadows at this time of year, and the river had never been known to rise above its banks.

It wasn't half coming down, though. He half-woke several times during the night, listening to the driving rain and wind, and each time thinking of the two boys. At dawn he got up and went to the window, relieved that at last the wind had dropped and the rain stopped. He drew back the curtains and looked down the valley. His own water meadows could not be seen, with the high bank in the way, but further down the valley the river twisted and wound its way to the sea. But now it was not just a river. As far as he could see, water had spread and covered banks, fields and pastures, a wide moving sheet instead of a winding ribbon.

The farmer's weariness dropped away. He sprang into life, pulling on his clothes and hurrying to pound on his son's bedroom door. 'Ben! Get up and get dressed, quick! River's flooded and those two young lads...'

Minutes later, the two of them, father and son, hurried from the back door into a wet, grey dawn. At the same moment, there came the sound of a car driving fast up the lane and turning into the farmyard.

* * *

Tom and Michael splashed their way through the water to the island where the marooned lamb stood alone. It had bleated for help until it was hoarse, and now stood deject-edly, head drooping, taking no notice even of its mother's frantic cries. The water was soon over the tops of the boys' boots. For a moment, Michael felt panic rise again. But then they had reached the knoll and grabbed the lamb.

On being rescued, the lamb came to life and began to struggle. It was amazing how heavy a wriggling small lamb could feel when you were wading with it through water to your knees. Weariness pressed heavy on Tom like a heavy weight. Michael was trying to hold part of the lamb, but couldn't get a grip on its kicking legs. 'I can manage it,' said Tom.

He could see that Michael was relieved. Michael's face was scratched and bruised and his eyes were heavy. He splashed and staggered through the water, as though it was more than enough to get himself along.

Under the water, the ground was uneven. Their feet stumbled and sloshed and slithered. Still looking at Michael, Tom saw him suddenly stumble and pitch forward as his foot went into a hollow. Michael flung up his arms, lost his balance and fell. The water closed over his head. 'Get up, quick,' gasped Tom, still struggling with the lamb.

Somehow, Michael could not get himself upright again. He floundered and splashed, spluttering in terror whenever his head broke the surface. Gradually, he was moving away from the bank, out towards the swollen river.

Tom dropped the lamb. He had reached water shallow enough for the lamb to be able to splash towards dry land and its mother. Michael's head and flailing limbs were moving away from him. Tom kicked off his waterlogged boots and flung himself after him, striking out in the muddy water. He saw Michael's head come up again, moving out into midstream. Then it disappeared. Tom trod water, frantically searching with his eyes. Michael's head came up again, nearer, his face white and terrified. Tom plunged towards him and grabbed for the hood of his anorak, floating on the surface. He groped desperately with the other hand for something solid to hold on to. Willows were half-submerged under the floodwater, and a branch drooped far enough for him to grab. For a moment he thought he would be pulled in two as the river surged and sucked, trying to drag Michael away from him.

'Mike,' he managed to splutter. 'Try and swim - over here - to me.'

Michael, terrified, fought a frantic urge to cling to Tom with all his might. He coughed water and struck out, feeling the weight of his boots pulling at his legs. But he was able to make the few strokes to bring his head level with Tom's. He grabbed the bending, straining willow branch and hung on with both hands.

Numb and tired as they were, the boys had no reserves of strength to get themselves out of the river. They clung desperately to the bending branch while the water gurgled and sucked at their legs. Their arms ached unbearably. Their strength ebbed. Tom knew that they could not hold on for long. Then the water would sweep them relentlessly out into midstream and away. He thought of Mum and Dad and Lucy, how it would be for them when the two bodies were washed up in the estuary or even out at sea.

He glanced sideways at Michael. He thought Michael looked half-drowned already, and terrified out of his wits. He was hanging on grimly though, gritting his teeth. Poor old Michael, thought Tom, he hadn't had much of a life. Suddenly he was determined that neither of them was going to be swept away and drowned.

He said, 'Hang on, Mike. We asked God to take care of us, didn't we?'

But he didn't know how long they could last out. Their whole bodies were numb and chilled. His arms ached and his eyelids kept drooping. It would be easy just to fall asleep... let go...

He saw that Michael's eyes were closing too. He said, 'Hang on, Mike,' in a kind of spluttering gasp. Michael's eyes fluttered open. They didn't know how much time had passed as they clung there under the river bank, treading water and gradually growing colder and weaker.

Suddenly there were voices above the roar of the water. Tom thought at first that Michael had spoken. He repeated weakly, once again, 'Hang on, Mike, hang on!'

But the voices were men's, more than one, and getting nearer. He raised his drooping head and tried to call out. But he could only manage a kind of feeble croak.

It didn't matter though, because one of the voices had risen to a shout. Next moment there were faces above them on the bank, and strong hands reaching down.

Michael was only dimly aware of being pulled out of the water and landed limp and half-drowned on the bank like a couple of fish. He slowly came to the knowledge that someone was pulling off his wet things, wrapping him in something warm, and that the feeling was painfully coming back to his numbed and chilled limbs.

He opened his eyes. Three large men in waterproof clothes were working hard over him and Tom. He saw that one was Mr Whitely from the farm and another seemed to be a younger edition of the farmer. The other, looking strained and pale, was more familiar.

'Dad!' croaked Michael, and struggled to rise from his half-sitting position. Dad knelt beside him and gathered Michael against his shoulder, stretching out his other arm to Tom. He heard Tom say, in a choked kind of voice, 'We saved the lamb, Dad. And all the camping stuff.'

Suddenly the tears that Michael had struggled for so long to hold back were overflowing and spilling hot down his cold cheeks. But it didn't matter any longer, for in spite of the mud and grime from the river water that covered both their faces, he saw that Tom was crying too.

Chapter Seventeen

'My Friend, My Brother'

It was mid-morning, and Tom and Michael, one in an outgrown bathrobe of Ben Whitely's, and the other in an ancient flannel dressing-gown, were tucked up snugly on a battered settee drawn close to the comfortable heat of Mrs Whitely's Aga cooker. Both had been soaked in hot baths, scrubbed and rubbed dry and given hot drinks, and their chills and shivering had stopped. Both felt pleasantly warm and very drowsy.

Dad came to sit in the big armchair opposite them. He said that Mrs Whitely was cooking a meal for them - a kind of breakfast-cum-early-lunch - and that after that they had both better get some sleep.

Tom thought that Dad was looking a bit tired himself, though none the worse for his bump on the head. He had rung Mum and Lucy, and given them a cautious account of what had happened, and assured them that everything was all right now.

'We won't have to go home, will we?' asked Tom drowsily. 'We can go on camping, can't we?'

Dad smiled, and said that Tom really was a glutton for punishment. 'I think, now the weather's changed, camping had better be out for these holidays.' Seeing Tom's face fall, he went on, 'But I've been talking to the Whitelys, and they've very kindly offered to have us here to stay at the farm, if we'd like to. They even suggested that Mum and Lucy come out too, for the second week of the holidays, as they've plenty of room.'

Tom brightened. In spite of everything that had happened he didn't want to go home yet. Then he remembered something that had been on his mind, and said, 'Dad, I'm sorry we didn't come here for the night like you wanted. I let Mr Whitely think I'd done a lot of camping. Michael and I might have drowned if you and the Whitelys hadn't come.'

Michael spoke up from his corner of the settee. 'No, we wouldn't. We asked God to take care of us in the tent, remember, Tom. And again in the water.'

Tom had forgotten. 'So we did.'

'I'm glad you remembered,' said Dad. 'You can be sure I prayed pretty hard myself, stuck there in the hospital, listening to that storm. I had a feeling you might try sticking it out at camp. Never dreamed the river would flood, though. God's been good, hasn't he?'

Both boys agreed. They were silent for a while, feeling sleepier and sleepier every minute. Michael's mind was still rather confused about it all, but a few facts seemed very clear. Michael needed Tom. Tom needed Michael. They both needed Dad - and other people, like the Whitelys. And all of them, even Dad, needed God their heavenly Father. He felt strangely content about it all.

Tom, too, felt at peace, and not just because of the warmth of the fire and the flannel dressing-gown, and the fact that they hadn't been swept away and drowned in the flooded river. Dad had told Tom that he and Mum had decided they really wanted to keep Michael for good, if everyone agreed. Tom did agree. In spite of everything - or maybe because of it - he felt it would be very hard to get along without Michael now.

Mrs Whitely came in, plump and cheerful, carrying a tray loaded with toast, scrambled eggs, crisp bacon, and a pot of steaming coffee. She put it down on a little table beside the boys.

'There now. You'll feel better with that inside you.'

She piled a plate with food and handed it to Tom, who suddenly felt ravenous. Filling another plate she glanced at Michael, whose head had fallen back and whose eyelids were drooping. She smiled at Tom. 'He's almost asleep, your friend.'

'My brother,' said Tom.

*If you enjoyed this book you will be pleased to know
that there are other books in the Fulmar series
from Christian Focus Publications.*

Find out more...

WINNER OF THE
CHILDREN'S BOOK CHALLENGE 1996

ARABELLA FINDS OUT

by Jacqueline Whitehead

'The screams and giggles were deafening and the whole place seemed full of wet hysterical children.

Arabella's father, hearing the noise from his study came outside. He looked in utter disbelief at what was going on and then shouted angrily at the top of his voice...for the first time in her life, Arabella felt frightened - everything was horribly out of control.'

Arabella hopes the party on her estate will impress her new friends. When her plans do not turn out as she expected she realises that being rich can cause problems. She begins to find out that her friends possess something which money can't buy. However, she is in for another shock when her father makes a terrible discovery...

£2.99 / ISBN 1-85792-161-5

Due to be published March 1996

Arabella was rich. In fact she was very, very, rich, at least her father was, and that meant she was too. At one time her father had been poor, but he didn't like it much. So he bought things that were cheap and nasty and sold them for too much money to anyone who would have them. Things like plastic Big Bens that played, "Maybe it's because I'm a Londoner", which were very popular with Japanese tourists, and Solar powered torches which were a big hit with Eskimos. Strangely enough, by selling things like these he became rich very quickly. By the time Arabella was born, he had quite forgotten what it felt like to be poor.

By the time Arabella was six she was quite used to telling off the servants, being rude to the gardeners and ordering Hargreaves the chauffeur to drive through enormous puddles just after he had spent all morning waxing the Bentley. Arabella didn't go to school but had a private tutor called Miss Marshall who came to the house on Mondays, Tuesdays, Thursdays and Fridays. On those days Arabella would go upstairs to the school room for her lessons. These were not a great success because when Miss Marshall said, 'Good Morning, Arabella, please open your books,' Arabella would shout, 'No, go and buy me some sweets.' Miss Marshall had a twitch.

When Arabella was nine her mother said to her one morning at breakfast, 'Darling, I think it is time you went to school.'

'What!' said Arabella.

'Don't say what,' said her father, his mouth full of buttered croissant and french coffee. 'Say pardon.'

Arabella glared at her father and shouted, 'What! What, what, what, what, what!' and pulled a face at him. Then she shrieked at her mother, 'I don't want to go to school, I want to stay at home with Miss Marshall.'

'Miss Marshall is not a very good teacher,' said her mother. 'What is three and three?'

'Eight,' yelled Arabella.

'Good grief,' said her father. 'It's definitely time you went to school.'

He was good at sums because he was used to counting all his money. He smiled at his wife. 'Have you a school in mind, my dearest?'

'Yes, I have,' she replied. 'Lady Worthington's Educational Establishment for rich, genteel young womenfolk.'

'Sounds ideal,' said Arabella's father. 'Why not give them a call after breakfast?'

'I did think we might take a drive over there this morning and have a chat with the head,' suggested Arabella's mother.

'Even better,' said Arabella's father warmly. 'It is Hargreaves' day off but I could drive us, it would make a pleasant change. We could stop and have lunch at Luigi's.'

'That's settled then,' said Arabella's mother, 'I'll go and get ready.'

'I don't think we had better take, 'you know who,' this time do you?' said Arabella's father nodding at Arabella in a very obvious way, but one which he clearly believed she wouldn't notice. Arabella's mother nodded back to show she agreed completely with the wisdom of this. 'We won't take you this time Snookums,' he said to Arabella, 'you can come and see your new school the next time we go.'

'Dadsy.' Arabella spoke in a soft wheedling tone. 'Snookums doesn't want to go to school.'

'I know,' he replied. 'But I'm afraid this time Snookums will have to trust that Mumsy and Dadsy know best.'

Arabella reverted to her old self.

'I don't want to go to school! I don't want to go to school! I don't want to go to school! I don't! I don't! I don't!' she screamed. After yelling blue murder for three minutes, holding her breath until she turned grey and threatening to be sick, Arabella gave up, realising this time Mumsy and Dadsy had made up their minds. How they must hate her to make her leave home every day to go to school.

Arabella flounced off feeling very cross and frustrated. No one understood her, no one cared, she didn't matter. As these thoughts took hold she began to feel very sorry for herself. Two big tears rolled down her cheeks and she stopped flouncing and became like a heroine in a tragedy. Suddenly with dramatic effect she flung an arm across her face and ran sobbing to the summer house in the east gardens hoping all the way that someone would see her performance and come to comfort her. There she threw herself to the floor and gave in to what she hoped was 'abandoned sobbing'. Arabella had read about it in a romantic book she'd found in Miss Marshall's bag when she was looking for peppermints and liked the sound of it. Miss Marshall never did find out where her book had gone, nor the peppermints for that matter.

Arabella sobbed as loudly as she could hoping all the time that her parents would hear and realise how cruel they were being but instead she heard the car start at the front of the house and pull away down the drive. She stopped sobbing. What a cheek they hadn't even come to say goodbye. She pouted sorrowfully, 'I'm all alone, with no one to care for me.' She said the words out loud and liked the feel of them. In fact there was a house full of staff, so she wasn't alone at all, but the thought suited Arabella's mood. At this she considered another bout of abandoned sobbing. As there was no one around to appreciate it she didn't bother and instead hauled herself up off the floor onto the wooden seat that ran round the inside of the summer house. Now what was she going to do? It was ages until lunch and she was bored already.

Arabella looked out of the summer house window across the gardens. In the distance she saw the sturdy timber fence that marked the east boundary of her family's property. She could see the outline of a five bar gate that she knew opened into a wood. The village was less than half a mile further on. Arabella had never walked down to the village on her own and she found herself wondering what it would be like. 'Only common, poor people walk anywhere,' said her mother and Arabella believed her.

As Arabella sat looking at the gate she had an idea. 'I know, I'll run away! I'll run away through that gate into those woods, then they'll be sorry. They'll soon wish they had never suggested school.' She stood up and in determined fashion strode out of the summer house and across the gardens heading towards the trees.

The woods wasn't a very accurate term for the little copse that stood just on the other side of Arabella's fence.

Many years before, it had been part of a great forest that stretched across the countryside but over the years this had been gradually cut away to make room for the village as it grew. Now there was little more than three or four rows of trees with thin stubbly undergrowth. In spite of this as Arabella came nearer to it she began to feel afraid. Her imagination caused the trees to grow huge and forbidding and she tried hard to remember if Miss Marshall had ever taught her about whether there were still bears in England or not. By the time she reached the gate she'd decided running away was not such a good idea after all and that she would rather have a drink and a doughnut instead. She turned to go back. It was then someone called, 'Hello,' causing Arabella to jump violently and squeal with fear.

'Who's there? Who is it?' she squeaked nervously, wishing with all her heart she hadn't come so far.

'It's only us,' said the voice. 'Sorry if we made you jump.'

'Who are you and what do you want?' Arabella looked, but could see nothing, then looking harder she realised there were two people hidden in the shadows of the wood, both so grubby and dirty they were almost the same colour as the trees...

Who is hiding in the shadows?
If you would like to find out what happens next,
this book will be available from Christian bookshops
from March 1996.

SAVE SAM

by Alistair Brown

Rescuing Sam, an abandoned puppy, gave Helen hope that she might at last have a dog of her own. But Sam is put in kennels, and Helen discovers he'll die in a week unless she can buy him back. With no money, saving Sam is impossible. Yet Helen knows he's meant to live.

The days tick away and Helen feels desperate. Then a wild storm brings a tree crashing to the ground, and Helen faces an even greater tragedy than the death of a puppy.

Meeting serious problems with only faith and prayer becomes very real for Helen.

£2.99 / ISBN 1-85792-021-X